W9-BRO-048

nickelodeon

PAW PATROL™

PUP, PUP, AND AWAY!

Based on the teleplay by Kim Duran
Illustrated by Harry Moore

A Random House PICTUREBACK® Book

Random House 🏠 New York

© 2015 Spin Master PAW Productions Inc. All rights reserved. Published in the United States by Random House Children's Books, a division of Random House LLC, 1745 Broadway, New York, NY 10019, and in Canada by Random House of Canada Limited, Toronto, Penguin Random House Companies. Pictureback, Random House, and the Random House colophon are registered trademarks of Random House LLC. PAW Patrol and all related titles, logos, and characters are trademarks of Spin Master Ltd. Nickelodeon and all related titles and logos are trademarks of Viacom International Inc.

randomhousekids.com
ISBN 978-0-553-50794-2
MANUFACTURED IN CHINA
10 9 8 7 6 5 4 3 2 1

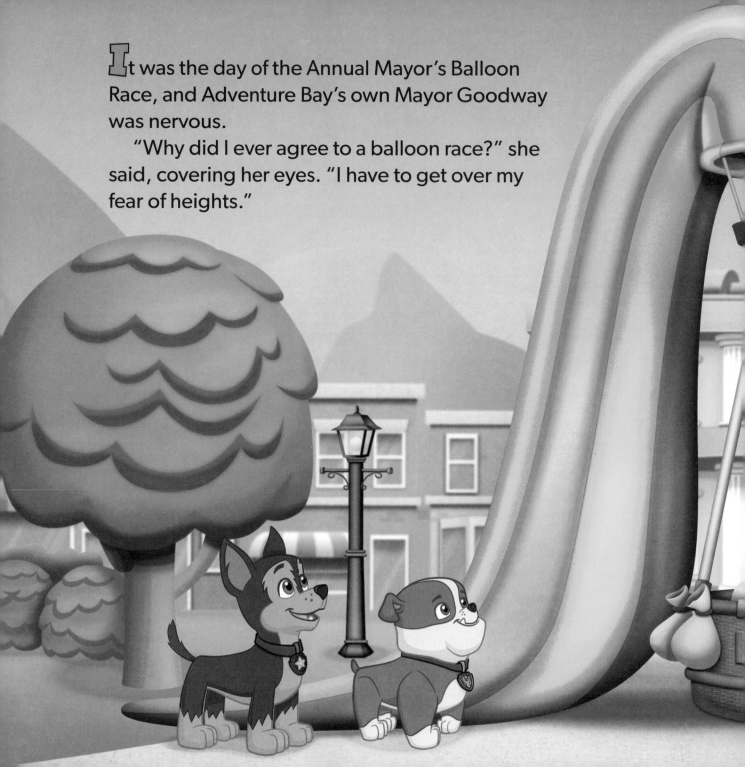

It was the day of the Annual Mayor's Balloon Race, and Adventure Bay's own Mayor Goodway was nervous.

"Why did I ever agree to a balloon race?" she said, covering her eyes. "I have to get over my fear of heights."

"Don't worry. I'll be in the balloon to help you," said Ryder. "Ready to unroll the balloon, pups?"
"We're ready!" Rubble barked.

Rubble and Chase unrolled the dusty balloon.
"Uh-oh!" Chase said. "It's got a . . . a . . . *ACHOO!*"
When he had stopped sneezing from the dust, he
continued, ". . . a hole! A ripped balloon can't hold air!"

Mayor Goodway groaned. "Mayor Humdinger from Foggy Bottom will win again!"

"Don't worry," Ryder said. "We'll get this balloon ready for the race. No job is too big, no pup is too small."

Ryder pulled out his PupPad and called the rest of the PAW Patrol.

The PAW Patrol quickly assembled at the Lookout. "Ready for action, Ryder, sir!" Chase barked.

Ryder told the pups about the mayor's balloon. "We need to fix the balloon for the race. Rocky, can you find something in your recycling truck that we can use to patch it?"

"Don't lose it, reuse it!" Rocky said.

"And the hot air that makes the balloon rise comes from a gas flame," Ryder continued. "Marshall, I'll need you to make sure the heater is safe."

"I'm all fired up!" Marshall exclaimed.

The PAW Patrol raced to the town square. Rocky quickly inspected the tear in the balloon. "I've got the perfect patch in my truck," he said.

"And how do the gas tanks look?" Ryder asked.

"The big question is how do they smell," Marshall replied. He sniffed the tanks. "I don't smell any gas leaks."

Rocky glued a piece of Zuma's old surf kite over the hole.
"Good work!" Ryder exclaimed. "That patch is a perfect fit."
Ryder turned a lever and the balloon slowly filled with hot
air. The other balloons were gathering on the horizon. The
race was about to begin.

"Time to get over my fear of heights!" the mayor shouted. "I'm going to win this race!"

She pumped her fist and accidentally hit the lever on the heater, flipping it all the way open. The balloon started to fly away!

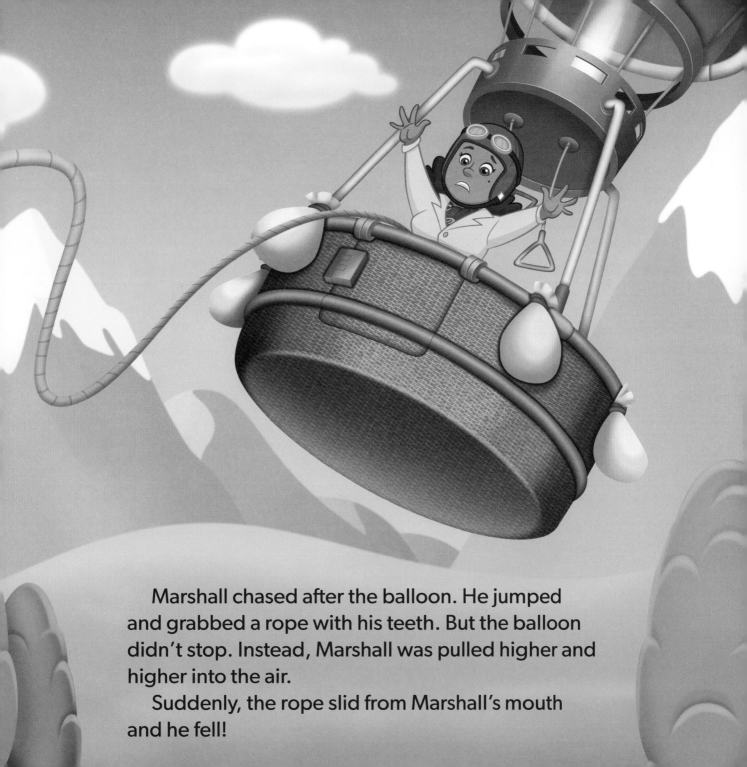

Marshall chased after the balloon. He jumped and grabbed a rope with his teeth. But the balloon didn't stop. Instead, Marshall was pulled higher and higher into the air.

Suddenly, the rope slid from Marshall's mouth and he fell!

Marshall landed right in Ryder's arms. "Thanks, Ryder!" he barked.

The race had started, and there was no time to waste. Ryder called Skye on his PupPad.

"Mayor Goodway took off without me! I need you to fly me to her balloon in your copter."

© Spin Master PAW Productions Inc. All rights reserved.

© Spin Master PAW Productions Inc. All rights reserved.

Skye slid into her Pup House, which quickly turned into a helicopter. "Let's take to the sky!" she exclaimed as she zoomed into the air.

Skye flew to Ryder and dropped a harness down to him. He locked himself in, and Skye whisked him away.

"I'll swing you over to the balloon," Skye said. But she had to hurry because the balloon was headed straight for the lighthouse on Seal Island!

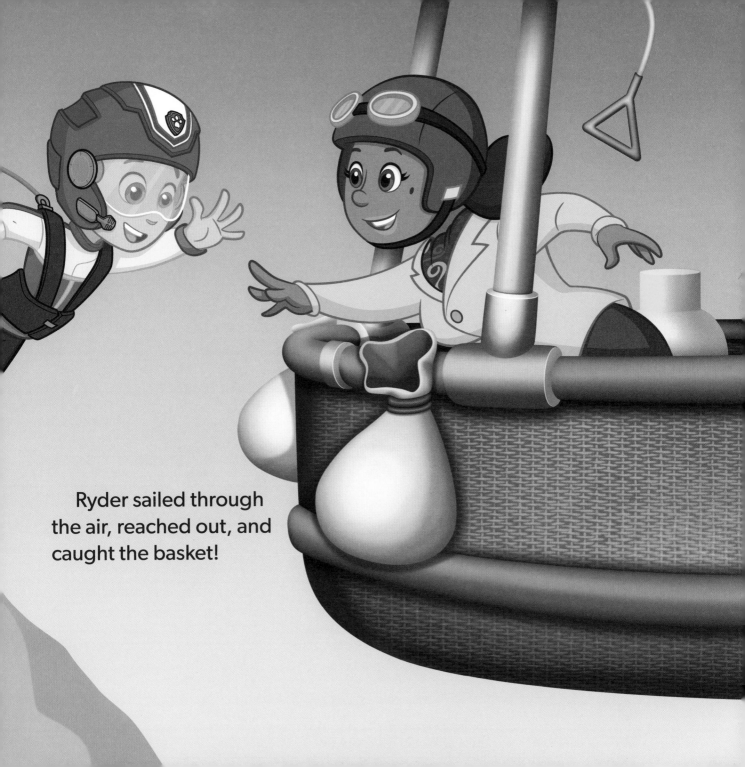

Ryder sailed through
the air, reached out, and
caught the basket!

Mayor Goodway helped Ryder climb into the balloon. He quickly gave it a burst of hot air and it rose over the lighthouse.

"Made it, Skye," Ryder reported as he undid his harness.

"Roger that!" Skye said, flying away. "Go win that trophy!"

"All right, Mayor Goodway, are you ready to win this race?"
The mayor gave Ryder a thumbs-up. "I'm in it to win it!
They raced after the other balloons.

With Ryder at the controls, the balloon quickly caught
up with Mayor Humdinger, who was in the lead.
"The race is on!" Ryder yelled.
"I've never lost a race, and I'm not starting now!"
Mayor Humdinger shouted back.

With a rush of hot air, Ryder and Mayor Goodway's
balloon whooshed past Mayor Humdinger.
"There's Jake's Mountain!" Mayor Goodway exclaimed.
"The finish line is on the other side!"

"The winds are stronger up high," Ryder said.
"We'll have a better chance of winning if we go up."
"Up, up, and away!" Mayor Goodway cheered.

Ryder guided the balloon higher and rode the rushing winds over Jake's Mountain—but Mayor Humdinger did the same! His balloon zipped right past Ryder and Mayor Goodway.

Down on the ground, all the PAW Patrol pups cheered as the balloons came into view. Mayor Humdinger's balloon swooped out of the sky first . . . but Mayor Goodway and Ryder dropped ahead of him at the last second and crossed the finish line. They won the race!

Mayor Humdinger sadly handed the trophy to Mayor Goodway. "I believe this belongs to you."

Mayor Goodway gave the trophy to Ryder.
"This belongs to Ryder and the PAW Patrol."
"Thanks, Mayor Goodway!" Ryder said with a smile.
"Whenever you need a hand, just yelp for help!"